Let's Talk Together

Home Activities for Early Speech & Language Development

by
Cory Poland, MA, CCC–SLP
&
Amy Chouinard, MA, CCC–SLP

Talking Child LLC
PO Box 2044
Maple Grove, MN 55311
www.TalkingChild.com

Talking Child LLC

©2008 by Talking Child LLC
PO Box 2044
Maple Grove, MN 55311
www.TalkingChild.com

Neither the author nor the publisher is responsible for injuries arising from the use or misuse of these materials. This includes, but is not limited to, failure to follow instructions and use of activities without consultation by a qualified speech-language pathologist. It is assumed that the speech-language pathologist is using, or supervising the use of, these materials is aware of any physical or cognitive limitations that might contraindicate their use with individual children.

Dedication

With love to our children:
Ally, Ana, and Charlie,
who bring us more joy than they could ever imagine.

Acknowledgements

We are deeply grateful to the following people who helped make this book possible:

Our husbands, Ian and Paul, for their unfailing love and support,

Our parents for their encouragement and the great amount of time they spent to help us,

and

Courtney Foster, Leann Latus, Amy Coe, Corri Stuyvenburg, Christine Dahl, Stacy Tepp, Jennifer Wollner and Kimberly Jones for their invaluable suggestions.

Contents

Introduction

Let's Talk Together is written by two speech therapists for the benefit of parents and caregivers who interact with a language-delayed beginning talker. This book is intended to be used as a supplement to professional speech therapy.

The activities in *Let's Talk Together* are based on the results of research and our own clinical experience. They provide a structure that you can follow with your child; you can teach, and your child can learn through interactive play rather than monotonous drills. Research has shown that teaching through interactive play is the most effective therapy approach (Greenspan & Wieder 1998). Many of the activities in this book require you to label objects in your child's environment which has been shown to boost speech development (Baxendale & Hesketh, 2003; Fey, et al., 1993). As a further example of how we incorporate proven research, this book includes activities that develop rhyming, which is a skill that most children must master before they can read (Pianta, 2004, p. 175).

Let's Talk Together includes our favorite language activities that take place in a child's natural environment – including but not limited to mealtime, indoor play, outdoor play, car time, and night time routines. Incorporating language-based activities into daily routines allows parents and caregivers opportunities for repetition and the flexibility to practice these activities at a time convenient for them. Presenting the activities in a fun but natural manner helps children relax so that they will be much more likely to participate.

How to Use This Book

The text in *Let's Talk Together* is divided into eight chapters. Each chapter identifies a routine experience in a young child's day such as "Meal Time" or "Indoor Play". Each chapter contains several individual activities that focus on target words and language objectives.

Individual activities may contain the following sections: Target of this Activity, Materials, Example Target Words, Rationale, and Procedure.

The Target of this Activity section clearly states the purpose or goal of each activity. Activities can be modified to focus on different goals.

The Materials section specifies which items are necessary to have on hand to complete the task.

The Example Target Words (or in some cases, Sounds) are divided into three groups of varying difficulty: beginning, simple, and difficult. This section is the most important part of the activity for two reasons: 1) it allows parents to practice target words that are appropriate for the child's level and 2) the same activities can be repeated at a more difficult level once the child successfully completes the initial objective.

Have you ever wondered why some late-talking children use very few words even though parents encourage words daily? Then one day a speech therapist sets up a therapy plan, plays with a child on a routine basis, and suddenly the child is adding new words to his vocabulary regularly. Often, the answer is the target words. Most children learn how to make sounds in a specific developmental order. Just as children learn to stand before they walk and run before they skip, most children learn to produce bilabial sounds (/p, b, m/) before they say more difficult velar sounds such as /k, g/. Thus, the word "boom" is commonly imitated before the word "crash". In most cases, if a child has not mastered the skill of standing, he will not attempt to walk on his own. Likewise, if a child has not mastered the more simple sounds and words, he will likely not attempt to say the more difficult ones.

Let's Talk Together includes sets of target words and sounds that are grouped by developmental norms. Thus, as a parent, you can consult your speech therapist to determine which target set to focus on for each activity. Then just play and have fun with your child! The rest has been planned for you.

The Rationale section is included on certain activity pages to provide further speech and language information for parents. It explains why the activity is important for development of language.

The Procedure is the final section and explains how the authors perform this activity. Feel free to adapt activities to better meet the needs of your child.

To use this book to help your child, find a couple of activities that your child enjoys. Consider the current level of your child to determine appropriate target words. Next, gather all the necessary materials. Incorporate the language-based activity in your child's day. Once you have completed the activity, encourage your child to imitate the same target words 3 or 4 times each day. Repetition throughout the day will have the greatest impact on your child. After he masters most of the beginning words feel free to repeat the activity and practice the simple words. After he masters most of the simple words then work on the difficult words. If you feel your child would benefit from more practice then find a different activity with similar or overlapping target words. Continue to practice the target words daily.

How many activities are recommended each week?

Our vision is that parents will choose one or two activities each week to complete with their child. Parents should then continue to reinforce these goals or target words several times a day throughout the rest of the week. It is our hope that, at a minimum, the target goals and words will be reinforced during the daily routine named in the chapter's title.

It is best to select a small number of target words and continue to reinforce them until they are mastered. Once your child has had success with those select words, move on to other words and other activities. Keep practice simple and consistent because you do not want to overwhelm or confuse your child.

What does /s/ mean?

Speech pathologists write phonemes in between two slashes. A phoneme is the smallest unit of a speech sound. For example, when you see that the target sound is /s/, that means the goal of the activity is to get your child to produce an "s" sound ("sss" like a snake). Likewise, /b/ refers to the "b" sound like those found in the words book and boat.

A Word About Safety

All of the activities in this book require adult supervision. Some activities may not be safe for all children. Every parent must use their own judgment in choosing which activities are safe for their own children. While Talking Child makes every effort to provide activities that are safe and fun; it is your responsibility to choose the activities that are safe in your own home. Please supervise your child when performing these activities, and prevent your child from accessing the items in the activities when you are not available to supervise.

About the use of "he"

For simplicity, male gender pronouns (he, him, his) will be used throughout this book to refer to your child.

About Talking Child

Talking Child was founded by two speech therapists. *The Baby Babble* video series and *Let's Talk Together* book were created with one goal in mind: to empower parents and caregivers so they can provide age-appropriate speech and language models for their beginning talkers. Talking Child's mission is to teach parents and caregivers how everyday activities with young children may become language-enriched, meaningful interactions. Please visit TalkingChild.com for more information.

A Note to Parents and Caregivers

Dear Parents,

The activities in *Let's Talk Together* are intended to be used as a supplement to speech therapy. If you suspect a delay in your child's speech development then you should consult a speech therapist (also called Speech Language Pathologist) who diagnoses and treats communication disorders. The speech therapist will evaluate your child. Depending on the results, the therapist may work with your child on a weekly basis or may suggest activities like those in *Let's Talk Together* that you and your child can do at home to improve his speech and language development.

A speech therapist usually works with a child for only a couple of hours each week. You, as the parent or caregiver, can dramatically boost your child's language skills by routinely engaging him in *Let's Talk Together's* short, structured activities throughout the entire day.

Just think, if you engage your child just one time a day with the language-enriched activities included in *Let's Talk Together*, your child's language environment will be enriched sevenfold! Ask your spouse to do the same and it jumps to 14-fold!

While these activities are created for you, the caregiver, and your child, the consultation with a speech therapist can be invaluable. A speech therapist that personally knows the needs and goals of you and your child will be able to lead you to activities in this book that will be the most beneficial and appropriate for your child.

A good speech therapist will incentivize development by rewarding verbal communication while teaching your child age-appropriate words, and engaging him in short and structured activities -- like the ones in *Let's Talk Together*.

Best of luck!

Cory and Amy

Refrigerator Reminders

Communication Tips for Parents of Young Children

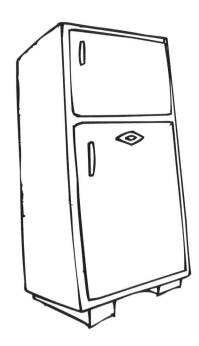

1) **Observe your child.** Pay attention to your child's vocalizations, gestures, eye gaze, and body movements. If you are playing blocks with your child and you notice his gaze moves to a bunny hopping across the yard, begin modeling simple words he could use to talk about the bunny such as "bunny" or "hop". Children want to share their interests with you so it is important to model the words they might use to talk about their interests.

2) **Get your child's attention before speaking.**
Call your child by his first name. Give him a few seconds to respond. Wait for your child to make eye contact with you. If your child does not respond then go over to him and say his name again while bending down to his level. Gently touch his arm or shoulder if necessary.

3) **Be specific.** "Clean up your room" or "Put your toys away" are directions that may not be clear to a young child. "Put the blocks back in the toy box" is a request that offers detailed information about what you would like your child to do.

4) **Shorter is better.** Young children have short memories so it is best to focus on one instruction at a time. Use short, clear sentences. "Put your blocks in the toy box, put on your shoes, and get in the car" is asking your child to remember three different things. In this situation, your child may begin to put the blocks away but then start playing with something else because he forgot the other two instructions. Instead, focus on one instruction at a time. "Erin, it's time to go. Please put on your shoes."

5) **Encourage verbalizations.** Children lose their motivation to communicate when parents react to non-verbal communication like pointing and gesturing. Whenever possible, wait for your child to express himself verbally before handing him what he wants.

6) **Select your words carefully.** Did you know that most children learn to say "Mama" before "Mommy"? "Mama" is easier for beginning talkers because the same syllable, "ma", is repeated. "Mommy" is more difficult because there is a vowel change which requires more motor planning for the mouth and articulators to change shape. Your child wants to please you. If your child does not imitate your target word it may be because the target word is too difficult for him to say. Choose sounds and words that are easy for your child to imitate.

7) **Avoid "What's this?"** In an effort to get a child to talk, we often observe parents pointing to pictures in a book and repeatedly asking, "What's this?" While in some cases, the drill technique may be beneficial (or recommended by a speech therapist) for sound practice, it does not teach the child how to engage in typical face-to-face interaction with turn taking. Instead, model words and phrases your child might enjoy saying. "Tractor, red tractor" and "Swing - the girl is swinging. Wee" are phrases your child may prefer to say.

8) **Know your child's limit.** Practice speech and language activities when your child is well-rested and happy. Many parents find the best time to work with their children is in the morning or after an afternoon nap. Be positive and encouraging so your child remains motivated. Children tend to "shut down" when they are tired, frustrated, or feel they cannot meet your expectations.

9) **Repeat often.** Young children benefit from short, repetitious activities. In most cases, it is better to practice twice a day for five minutes than once a day for fifteen minutes.

10) **Be consistent.** Your speech therapist will help you come up with a list of target words that are appropriate for your child. Incorporate the target words into your child's routine activities each day. Be patient and consistent! You will be amazed at how your child's communication abilities evolve over time.

Chapter 1

Activities for Beginning Sounds

Ooo-Ahh Game

Target of This Activity

This activity is designed to encourage your child to imitate and vocalize beginning speech sounds.

Materials

Mirror (optional)

Example Target Words

Beginning Vowels	Simple Vowels	Difficult Vowels
Ooo (as in t<u>oo</u>) Ahh (as in c<u>a</u>t) Eee (as in b<u>ee</u>) Oh (as in n<u>o</u>)	Ooo–eee Eee–ooo Eee–ahh Ahh–ooo Eee–ooo Uh–oh	E-I-E-I-O (as sung in *Old McDonald Had a Farm*)

Rationale

In typical language development, children imitate vowel sounds first. This stage is called cooing and gooing. Once children learn to coo and goo, they babble by adding simple consonants (like /p, b, m/) to vowels ("ba-ba-ba", "ma-ma-ba", "ba-pa-ma"). These babbles are shaped into meaningful environmental sounds ("baa baa" for sheep, "moo moo" for cow).

After children learn to babble and produce environmental sounds, they begin to say their first words.

We believe it is important to practice vowel sounds because children learn how to phonate. Further, they are the simplest speech sounds to produce. Vowels are produced by opening the mouth while phonating. Phonation is the result of vibrating the vocal folds while supplying airflow.

Procedure

To begin this activity, sit with your child facing you. Exaggerate your mouth movements as you say various vowel sounds such as "ooo", "eee", "ahh", and "oh". Encourage your child to imitate you. For added complexity, combine vowel sounds such as "ooo–eee", "eee–ahh", "oh–eee", "eee–oh", "eee–ooo", "oh–ahh", and "ahh–oh". Continue to encourage your child to imitate you. Do not get discouraged if your child does not try to imitate you. He is still taking it all in! Once he is imitating the vowel sounds you make, sing songs like *Old McDonald Had a Farm*. Encourage your child to sing "E-I-E-I-O".

Animal Play

Target of This Activity

This activity is designed to teach your child how to produce animal sounds and first words during playtime.

Materials:

Paper plate or brown paper bag

Construction paper

Glue

Scissors

Markers

Puppet template (optional) available at TalkingChild.com

Example Target Words

Beginning Sounds	Simple Words	Difficult Words
Moo (cow)	Pony	Sheep
Baa (sheep)	Puppy	Horse
Neigh (horse)	Bird	Cat
T(w)eet (bird)	Dog	Chick
Wuh (dog)	Owl	Cow
Peep (chick)		Pig
Hoo (owl)		

Procedure

Most children begin saying animal sounds and environmental sounds shortly before they speak their first words. Below are some ideas for encouraging these sounds.

Animal Puppets: Create animal puppets using a brown paper bag or paper plate and construction paper. Each time you glue on a piece of paper, encourage your child to say the corresponding animal sound. Put on a puppet show and have the animals say their sounds using sentence-like intonation as they "talk" to each other.

Sing a Song: Place animal puppets or animal figures in a bag. Sing *Old MacDonald Had a Farm* with your child. Each time it is time to name an animal, allow your child to reach into the bag and pull out an animal.

Animal Peek-a-boo: Choose an animal puppet and hold it behind a couch or door. Pop the puppet out from behind the door and say the appropriate animal sound. Repeat a few more times and then tell your child it is his turn. Act very startled and surprised when your child peeks the animal puppet around the door to encourage more repetitions. Smile, and say, "Oh... you surprised me! You said, 'moo.'"

Cereal Stack - "Oh"

Target of This Activity

This activity is designed to teach
your child how to imitate first words.
This activity is also beneficial for
developing fine motor skills.

Materials

Any round cereal (Cheerios™,
Honeycomb™, Froot Loops™, etc.)

Frosting

Paper plate

Example Target Words

Beginning Words	Simple Words	Difficult Words
Oh	1,2,3 (counting)	Cheerios™
Uh-oh	Down	Honeycomb™
Mmm	Whoa!	Fruit Loops™
More	On top	Tower
Eat		Yummy
		Fall Down!

Procedure

Below are some entertaining activities involving round cereals. Parents can engage children both at home and restaurants while waiting for their meals.

Cereal Tower: Sit at a table with your child. Give your child a pile of round cereal. Show your child how to stack one piece of cereal on top of another one. Model "oh" for your child as you place each cereal piece on top of the tower. Next time, delay and see if your child will spontaneously imitate you by saying "oh". See how many round cereal pieces you can put on the tower before it falls down. Practice saying "uh-oh" once your child has knocked the tower down. Children love to knock down the tower and eat them too! "Mmm, yummy!"

"O" Fun: Cut a hole in the middle of a paper plate so that it looks like the letter "o". Place a pile of round cereal on a different plate with a little frosting off to the side. Show your child how to dip his finger into the frosting and put some on a round cereal piece. "Mmm, yummy!" The frosting acts as glue. Next, stick the frosting-covered cereal piece onto the paper plate. Add more cereal pieces until the plate is covered. Hold the paper plate in the air upside down and see if the cereal will "fall down". Alternatively, create an oral motor activity by trying to get the cereal pieces off of the plate with just a tongue and no hands.

Beginning Language Games

Target of This Activity

This activity is designed to teach your child to imitate gestures and simple words.

Materials

Napkin

Example Target Words

Beginning Words	Simple Words	Difficult Words
Boo	Peek	Pat-a-cake
Pat	Cake	Peek-a-boo!
More	Bake	Roll
Big	So big!	My turn
		Your turn

Rationale

The games below encourage language development, object permanence, and social play. Object permanence is an important stage in child development (typically developed around 8-9 months) in which a child develops an awareness that objects continue to exist even when they are no longer visible. Peek-a-boo is a common game that practices this skill.

Procedure

Peek-a-boo: Cover your head with a napkin or cover your eyes with your hands. Pause. Uncover and say, "Peek-a-boo!" At first your child might be concerned as you "disappear" behind the napkin or your hands. When you reappear, his face will likely be delighted and elated with joy. Encourage your child to hide his face, then uncover it and say "Boo!"

Pat-a-cake: Sit with your child facing you. Say the following nursery rhyme in a sing-song fashion. Accompany the words by hand-clapping. Alternate between a normal clap and patting your lap (thighs) with your hands.

> Pat-a-cake, pat-a-cake, baker's man.
>
> Bake me a cake as fast as you can (clap hands, pat lap).
>
> Pat it (pat lap) and roll it (roll hands) and mark it with a "B" (make "B" in air with finger)
>
> And put it in the oven for baby and me! (Point to child and then to you.)

Repeat the rhyme a few times and then see if your child will initiate the game by clapping. Say "Your turn!" Encourage your child to imitate the gestures and sing or hum along.

Who's so big?: While your child is sitting in a high chair or booster seat, ask, "Who's so big?" Then raise your hands over your head and say, "So big!" Repeat the activity and see if your child will imitate you by gesturing or saying, "So big!" Encourage your child to imitate you by gently raising his hands in the air while modeling, "So big!"

Imitating Actions and Sounds

Target of This Activity

This activity is designed to motivate your child to imitate sounds and words, as well as teach pretend play skills.

Materials

Blanket

Safety pin

Example Target Words

Beginning Words	Simple Words	Difficult Words
Zoom! Wee!	Hop Go Jump	Ready, set, go! Blanket Cape Run Spin

Rationale

Gross motor or full body movement often encourages vocalizations. It is essential that your child begin to imitate you in order to learn to speak. If a child is unwilling to imitate speech sounds, first work on encouraging him to imitate body movements or gestures.

Procedure

Many children love copying mom and dad as they run around the house with a cape. Show your child how to create his own cape with a blanket. Then run down the hall and see if your child can do the same. Spin around in a circle. Encourage him to imitate you. Jump up and down or stand on one foot.

If your child does something unique, imitate him. Continue copying each other's movements. Once your child is imitating movements consistently, add some sounds. Run around the room and say "Zoom!" Encourage your child to imitate your sounds. Run around the room and say "Wee!" See if he will imitate your actions and sounds during this fun game!

In and Out Play

Target of This Activity

This activity is designed to encourage your child to babble, produce environmental sounds, or say words during independent play.

Materials

Toy cars

Toy trucks

Toy bus

Example Target Words

Beginning Words	Simple Words	Difficult Words
Ba-ba-ba	Vroom!	Crash!
Beep	Zoom!	Truck
Toot	Bus	Car
Boom	Go!	Stop!
Uh-oh	Push	
Wee!		

Rationale

Parents of late talkers often notice that their child is quiet during playtime. They report that he does not babble, say sounds, or say words while playing on his own.

This activity is designed to encourage your child to vocalize during independent play. Vocalizations during play are instrumental in your child's language development because he is able to practice sounds and words on his own. Children do not learn to walk independently on the first try. It takes a lot of practice. Likewise, learning to talk takes practice.

Procedure

Place some toy cars and trucks in a play area for your child. Sit on the floor with your child. Push the cars around and say "beep beep". Encourage your child to do the same. Show your child how to push the car quickly and say "vroom vroom". Make the cars crash into each other and say "uh-oh".

If your child is not yet saying environmental sounds like "vroom," model beginning sounds. Say "ba-ba-ba" as you push the car around the room.

Over time, your child will begin to vocalize while you play with him. This is "In Play" because you are in the room playing with him. After your child has been vocalizing with you for a few minutes, it is time to see if he can vocalize during independent play. Slowly move back away from your child so that you are sitting three to four feet away from him. Allow him to play on his own for a few minutes.

If your child's vocalizations decrease, model sounds and words for him. If your child continues to vocalize while playing for four to five minutes, stand up and walk out of your child's play area to the edge of the room. This is called "Out Play".

Watch your child play for a few minutes on his own. If he becomes quiet and less talkative, walk back into his play area. Continue to model the sounds and words for him as he plays. Continue "In and Out Play" with your child daily. This will help your child learn to vocalize independently during play.

Babble Parade

Target of This Activity

This activity is designed to encourage your child to make vocalizations.

Materials

Pots and pans

Wooden and metal spoons

Whistles

Bells

Tambourines

Bubbles

Flags/streamers

Example Target Words

Beginning Words	Simple Words	Difficult Words
Ba-ba-boom Da-da-doom Ma-ma-ma Boom	Bang Pot Lid Bubble Bell	We're in the parade My turn Your turn March! Spoon Drum

Procedure

Kids love music, banging, and marching! Ask playgroup members or siblings to participate in your parade. Give each participant one of the items listed above. Get in a line and march around your house. Alternatively, march on the sidewalk in your neighborhood. Show your child how to play the "drum" (pot). As you are marching and making music, say "ba-ba-boom". See if your child will imitate you.

Say a sound each time you hit the drum or tambourine. Exaggerate these sounds. Encourage your child to imitate the words and sounds that you say.

Now it is your child's turn to be the leader. Encourage him to say sounds or words. Imitate the sounds and words he says. Encourage the other children in the parade to imitate your child as well. While marching, say a chant such as, "March! March! March! March! We're in the big parade!"

Trade instruments and encourage your child to say "my turn" or "your turn".

Toy Talk

Target of This Activity

This activity is designed to teach your child to vocalize various environmental and animal sounds.

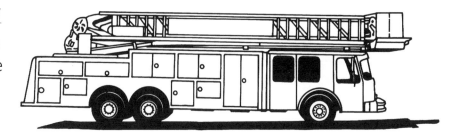

Materials

Toy farm set including animals and barn

Toy firetruck and police car

Toy phone

Example Target Words

Beginning Words	Simple Words	Difficult Words
Moo (cow)	Beep (microwave)	Brrng (telephone ringing)
Hoo (owl)	Toot (car)	Oink (pig)
Peep (chick)	Eee-ooo-eee-ooo	Plop (water dripping)
Baa (sheep)	(firetruck siren)	Rib-bit (frog)
Wuh (dog)	Neigh (horse)	Quack (duck)
Ah–ah–ah–ah (police siren)		

Procedure

Children hear many sounds throughout the day. Birds chirping, leaves rustling, sirens blaring, airplanes flying, phones ringing, and dogs barking are just a few.

While playing with your child, demonstrate various sounds that objects (toys) and animals make in our world. Add appropriate sounds to as many toys as you can. Encourage your child to imitate your sounds or make up his own.

Farm Sounds: While playing with a farm set, make the appropriate animal sound as you walk each animal into the barn. See if your child will imitate you. Say, "Moo, the cow says moo! You do it. Moo, moo!"

Siren Sounds: While playing with a police car or firetruck, make a siren sound out of exaggerated vowel sounds. Start slowly and speed up your siren sound. See if your child will imitate you.

House Sounds: Walk around the house with your child and pay attention to the sounds that you hear. Say "brrng" while passing the toy telephone. Press a button on the microwave and say "Beep!" Listen to water drip from the faucet and say "Plop!" Encourage your child to imitate each sound he hears.

Chapter 2

Oral Motor Activities

Oral motor activities (i.e. exercises for the mouth) can increase oral awareness as well as increase strength, range of motion, and coordination of oral musculatures (i.e. lips, tongue, jaw) for speech production and feeding skills.

Blowing Activities

Target of This Activity

This activity is designed to teach your child how to blow correctly while encouraging lip protrusion and lip rounding.

Materials

Mirror

Cotton balls

Straw

Cup of water

Bubbles

Rationale

As speech pathologists, we believe that learning how to blow correctly is important for speech development. Blowing encourages sustained breath support which is needed for connected speech (talking in sentences). Further, it helps strengthen the muscles needed for speech. It also teaches lip puckering (protrusion) and lip rounding – which are two oral motor positions common to many speech sounds.

Ask your child to blow some bubbles. While your child is blowing bubbles, observe his technique. Is he blowing air in a smooth, uniform pattern? Are his lips protruded as if he is giving a kiss? Are his lips rounded or are they tense and flat?

Procedure

Below are some motivating activities that can be used to teach your child to blow correctly.

Mirror: Position your mouth so that you are one or two inches away from a mirror and say "hhha". Watch the mirror fog up as you speak. Encourage your child to try. Once he can do this, ask him to softly say "hooo" next to the mirror to work on lip rounding.

Bubbles: Blow a bubble, catch it on the bubble wand, and see if your child can kiss the bubble. (This works on lip protrusion and rounding – the precursor to blowing). Next, see if he can blow the bubble off the wand. If he has trouble, see if he can blow it off by softly saying "hooo". Finally, see if your child can make a bubble by blowing a bubble through the wand.

Straw: Submerge the bottom end of a drinking straw into a cup of water. Show your child how to make bubbles by blowing into the straw. If your child sips the water rather than blowing, take the straw out of the water and hold your child's hand a couple of inches away from the end of the straw. Blow through the straw and allow your child to feel the airflow on his hand. Now let your child try.

Cotton Balls: Place a cotton ball on the table and see if your child can blow it off the opposite edge. Once your child can do this, have cotton ball races! Sit at one end of the table together. Now see who can blow the cotton ball off the opposite edge of the table first.

Chapter 2: Oral Motor Activities

Oral Motor Practice with Whistles

Target of This Activity

This activity is designed to strengthen speech musculature while working on muscle memory, lip positioning, and tongue positioning.

Materials (To see pictures of the whistles, visit TalkingChild.com)

Siren whistle

Train whistle

Slide whistle

Airplane whistle

Rationale

We recommend blowing whistles because of the shape and size of the whistle's mouth piece. Each whistle we recommend requires the child to put his tongue and lips in a specific position consistent with certain speech sounds.

The key is to have the child blow the whistle for 10–15 repetitions. In between each rep, remove the whistle from the child's mouth and then immediately reinsert the whistle. This helps the child develop muscle memory for skills such as opening and closing the mouth, rounding and unrounding the lips, as well as protruding and retracting the tongue. For more information or to see pictures of the whistles described below, please visit our website at TalkingChild.com.

Procedure

Siren Whistle: The siren whistle helps stimulate vowels such as "ah" as in c<u>a</u>t, "ih" as in s<u>i</u>t, "eh" as in b<u>e</u>t, and "uh" as in c<u>u</u>t.

Train Whistle: The train whistle helps with lip closure and stimulates beginning sounds such as /p, b, m/.

Slide Whistle: The slide whistle teaches beginning lip rounding and lip closure. It also stimulates sounds such as "oo" as in b<u>oo</u>t, "oh" as in b<u>oa</u>t, and /w/.

Airplane Whistle: The airplane whistle helps practice tongue retraction and lip rounding. It also stimulates sounds such as "oo" as in b<u>oo</u>t, and /w, t, d, s, z/.

Other Ideas: Ensure your child is sitting up straight in a chair to supply proper breath support.

Hold the whistle in place for your child to ensure that he does not bite down on the mouthpiece. If your child is using his teeth to hold the whistle in place, pull the whistle out so that it does not protrude as far into his mouth and remind him to hold the whistle in his mouth with his lips.

Silly Faces

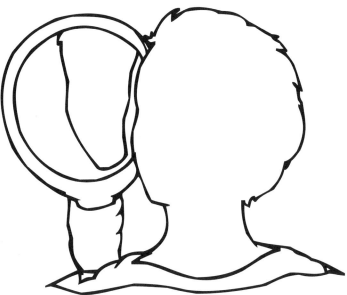

Target of This Activity

This activity is designed to see if your child can coordinate oral motor movements used in the production of speech. These oral exercises require tongue, lip, and jaw strength/control. Further, it is designed to teach your child to follow one-step commands.

Materials

Mirror

Straw

Procedure

Provide a visual model for your child during this activity. Ask your child, "Can you do this?" Show your child what you want him to do. Have a mirror accessible so that your child has some visual feedback during this activity.

Mouth Exercises:

Open mouth wide

Produce a sound ("ah" as in cat)

Close mouth

Blow through a straw (have child hold hand at the end of the straw to feel the air stream).

Breathe on a mirror with your mouth open. Ask your child if he can make the mirror foggy by saying "hhha".

Lip Exercises:

Smile

Blow a kiss (pucker lips)

Lip smacks

Tongue Exercises:

Protrude tongue (stick tongue out)

Lateralize tongue to the right (tongue to corner of mouth)

Lateralize tongue to the left (tongue to corner of mouth)

Try to touch tongue to nose

Try to touch tongue to chin

Retract tongue

Tongue clicks (click tongue on roof of mouth just behind the front teeth)

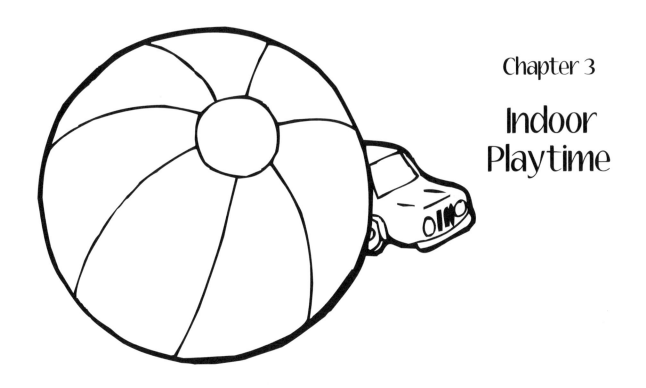

Chapter 3

Indoor Playtime

Ball Play

Target of This Activity

This activity is designed to teach your child turn taking skills and verbalizing simple requests.

Materials

Ball

Example Target Words

Beginning Words	Simple Words	Difficult Words
Ball	Go!	Your turn
More	Push	My turn
Oops	Stop	Ready, set, go!
Wee	Got it!	
Uh-oh		

Procedure

Sit on the floor with your legs stretched out and have your child sit across from you about five feet away. Take turns rolling a ball back and forth across the floor. Model words like "ball", "more", "go", and "your turn". Lift your leg a few times and allow the ball to roll under your knee. Say, "Oops, got it!"

Create opportunities for your child to verbalize. For example, before you roll the ball to him say, "Ready, set, ___." Pause dramatically while looking at your child with anticipation. Once your child attempts to verbalize, roll the ball immediately. Say "go" if your child does not respond within a few seconds. Continue taking turns rolling the ball back and forth and encourage him to say some of the target words listed above.

Other Ideas:

- An additional adult can sit behind your child and help him roll the ball or model turn taking.

- Encourage your child to use sign language (or a gesture that both of you understand) if he cannot say the words listed above.

- Older children may enjoy taking turns bouncing the ball instead of rolling it.

Block Tower

Target of This Activity

The goal of this activity is to encourage your child to talk during everyday play activities (even when you are not directly playing with your child).

Materials

Toy blocks

Example Target Words

Beginning Words	Simple Words	Difficult Words
Uh–oh	On top	Crash
On	Oops	More blocks
Boom	Counting (1, 2, 3…)	Block, please
Whoa	Block	Fall down
More	Tall	Tower

Procedure

Kids love stacking blocks. There are so many opportunities for language while they do this! Count the blocks, put them on top of one another, and see how many you can stack until they fall over. Use intonation while saying "boom", "uh-oh", and "whoa". Talk about the blocks as your child builds a tower by modeling, "on top", "more blocks", or "fall down".

Once your child begins to talk and imitate you as he plays, move away from him a little bit. See if you can encourage him to continue talking even though you are not actively involved in the activity. Ideally your child will begin to use the words that you modeled for him on his own. This "self talk" during play is a huge step toward further language development. It allows for more practice throughout the day and is a beginning step toward imaginative play, which is important for brain development.

Other Ideas:

- Keep the blocks in your lap and encourage your child to ask for "more".
- See if your child can build a tower that is taller than he is.
- See if your child can knock the tower down without touching it by blowing on it.
- See if your child can pretend to be the tower, swaying back and forth until it falls down!

Hide and Seek

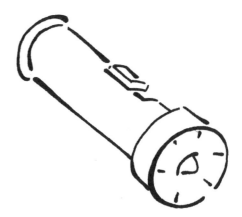

Target of This Activity

This activity is designed to motivate children to walk around a room, identify one object, and say its name. It is a motivating activity designed to hold a child's attention during multiple repetitions of the same word.

Materials

Flash light

5-7 pictures of an object

Bag

Special hat (optional)

Example Target Words

Beginning Words	Simple Words	Difficult Words
Moo (cow)	Baby	Book
Baa (sheep)	Apple	Bus
Neigh (horse)	Bubble	Car
Mama	Puppy	Tree
Dada	Open	Balloon

Procedure

Collect 5-7 pictures of the same object. Cut the pictures out of a magazine, print them from clip art on the computer, or develop a picture taken with a camera. For example, use multiple copies of a picture containing an apple. Alternatively, use pictures containing different apples (a green apple, a red apple, an apple on a tree, etc.). Hide the pictures around the house – next to the sofa, under the window, on a stair step, etc. Close the blinds and turn the lights down. Put on special treasure hunting hats and grab a flashlight! Say the following chant:

> We are going on a treasure hunt,
>
> A treasure hunt,
>
> A treasure hunt,
>
> We are going on a treasure hunt,
>
> Oh, what will we find?

Help your child use the flashlight to locate the hidden pictures. Once he finds each picture, say, "Yeah! You found it!" Say the object's name, and put it in a bag. Once all the pictures have been found, sit down with your child and pull the pictures out one by one. Count them and label them (so that your child has more opportunities to practice naming the picture).

Other Ideas:

- Focus on themes or categories. Hide pictures of objects that are the same shape or the same color.
- Hide real objects instead of pictures. Some examples are pretend food (apple, juice, cookie), toy cars (dump trucks, little and big cars), and balls (all sorts of shapes and sizes).

Bouncing Jelly Bean Song

Target of This Activity

This activity is designed to help your child identify body parts, make eye contact, learn gender concepts, and answer questions by pointing.

Materials

Big bouncy ball (yoga ball works well)

Example Target Words

Beginning Words	Simple Words	Difficult Words
Ball	Knee	Elbow
Eyes	Tummy	Arm
Head	Leg	Ankle
Toes	Ears	Wrist
Nose	Hand	Mouth

Procedure

(as sung to *The Farmer in the Dell*)

Help your child sit on a large ball. (Stabilize the ball by propping it in a corner and hold onto your child.) Bounce your child and sing:

> A jelly bean has no hair,
>
> A jelly bean has no hair,
>
> High-ho the derry-oh,
>
> A jelly bean has no hair!

Ask your child to point to his hair. When he does, say, "You're not a jelly bean, you're a boy/girl!" Continue the song, using different body parts (eyes, ears, mouth, foot, etc.). The repetitive bouncing movement usually excites children and the gross motor movements encourage them to verbalize.

Cars and Trucks

Target of This Activity

This activity is a repetitive activity designed to give your child many opportunities to correctly produce the target words.

Materials

Toy car

Example Target Words

Beginning Words	Simple Words	Difficult Words
Beep	Honk	Ready, set, go!
Toot	Go	Crash
Boom	Car	Fast
Vroom		Slow
Wee		Truck

Rationale

In speech development, young children generally perfect their pronunciation of new words through repetition. For example, a child learning to say the word "open" might first produce approximations such as "oh", "oh-ba", or "oh-pa" before correctly pronouncing "open".

Because young children tend to lose interest in repetitive exercises, the target of this activity is to turn repetition into a game. The two keys to success with this activity are to (1) start with target words that are the appropriate level for your child and (2) continue to focus on the same target words until your child has mastered them.

Procedure

Sit on the floor across from your child. Practice pushing a toy car back and forth across the room. See if your child can push it back to you. If your child has trouble taking turns pushing it back and forth, ask another adult or older sibling to play. This allows you to sit behind your child and help him send and receive the car.

As you play with your child, model words like "wee", "beep", "toot", and "honk". Once your child pushes the car back and forth consistently, say, "Ready, set, go!" Practice this a few times and then say, "Ready, set..." and then pause and wait in anticipation for your child to say "go". See if your child will say "go" or make some type of gesture.

Modify the target word based on the Example Target Word levels listed above. For instance, your child could say "wee" instead of "go" if working on the first level.

Computer Time

Target of This Activity

The goal of this activity is to teach your child early computer skills while encouraging interactive verbalizations.

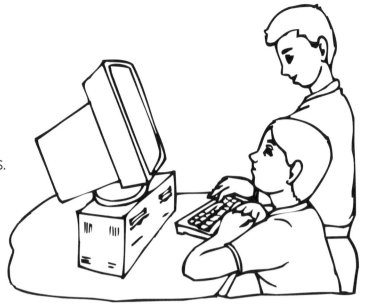

Materials

Computer with internet connection

Webcam (optional)

Example Target Words

Beginning Sounds	Simple Words	Difficult Words
Bzz (bee)	Puppy	Dinosaur
Baa (sheep)	Bee	Snake
Moo (cow)	Dog	Tiger
Meow (cat)	Cat	Elephant
Wuh (dog)	Bird	Zebra
Neigh (horse)	Duck	Alligator

Procedure

Below are some language-based computer activities that are very motivating for young children.

Picture Hunt: Use a computer with internet access and ask your child to sit on your lap. Go to the Google™ or Yahoo™ homepage to look for pictures of animals. For example, Google.com allows you to search solely for images if you click on the "images" link located above the search box. Type in an animal such as tiger, duck, dinosaur, or snake and watch as a plethora of images matching your search criteria appear. Practice the sounds that each animal says as you find its picture. Talk about the animal in the picture. Ask your child to point to the (animal name) with an open mouth, or point to the animal that is running (eating, walking, or sleeping). Work on categorizing skills by asking questions such as, "Which animal lives at a farm?" or "Which animal eats worms?"

Free Online Games: Did you know there are websites with fun interactive games for children as young as one year old on the internet? These sites and games can teach your child cause and effect, vocabulary words, beginning computer skills, letters, numbers, and phonics. An additional bonus is watching your child "light up" and talk to the monitor while playing the games. Go to www.TalkingChild.com for a list of our favorite online games for young children. Our list is organized by age to make the games easy to find.

Webcam: Allow your child to see himself on the computer monitor using a webcam. Encourage him to talk and make silly faces so he can see and hear himself talk. Alternatively, allow your child to use a webcam to talk with a close friend or family member. This encourages taking turns, eye contact, and verbalizations.

Dress Up

Target of This Activity

This activity is designed to teach your child two-word phrases while developing pretend play skills.

Materials

Dress up clothes

Example Target Words

Beginning Words	Simple Words	Difficult Words
Ah-hah-hah (belly laugh)	Tea	Want tea?
Hee-hee-hee (tiny mouse laugh)	Hat	Next stop
Eee-ooo-eee-ooo (police siren)	Out	Good day
	Oh no!	Help cat
Silly faces (for oral motor and imitation)	Up	Slow down
	Bye-bye	All-aboard!
	Hi	Ticket, please

Procedure

Dress up as a clown, fireman, princess, or train engineer. Decorate homemade hats to go with each costume. Use words associated with each profession. Encourage your child to use two-word phrases while playing.

Clown: Tape different colors of construction paper onto a hat and make funny faces in a mirror. (Examples: stick out your tongue, make air-filled cheeks, or fish face lips.) Wear daddy's shoes around the house. Practice different kinds of laughs. Teach your child how to make a big belly laugh ("ah-hah-hah"), or a tiny mouse laugh ("hee-hee-hee").

Fireman: Wear suspenders, a big coat, and a fire hat. Model the following sounds, words, and phrases for your child: "swish" (pretend to squirt water), "eee-ooo" (siren sound), "Oh no!", "cat in tree", "help cat", "cat down", and "all better".

Princess: Wear a dress, fancy shoes, and jewelry. Model the following sounds, words, and phrases: "Want tea?", "yes, please", "thank you", "More tea?", "mmm, yummy", "all done", and "no, thank you".

Train Engineer: Wear overalls and a hat. Model the following sounds, words, and phrases: "hi", "all-aboard", "next stop", and "ticket, please".

Indoor Winter Wonderland

Target of This Activity

This indoor activity is designed to teach your child about winter fun while learning new vocabulary, body parts, and adjectives.

Materials

Winter clothing such as gloves, mittens, hats, and scarves

Mirror

Cotton balls

Sled

Example Target Words

Beginning Words	Simple Words	Difficult Words
Brr (cold)	Boot	Snow
Up	Head	Sled
Down	Hand	Fast
Hat	Coat	Slow
Wee	Go out!	Scarf
	Ice	Mitten
	1, 2, 3 (counting)	

Procedure

Set out a variety of winter gloves, mittens, hats, and scarves for your child. Encourage your child to try on the items and look in the mirror. Pretend to "go out" and play in the snow. Use cotton balls and practice throwing, scooping, and putting the "snow" into piles.

Place cotton balls on the table and take turns blowing them off the edge. Have your child sit under the table and watch it "snow" as the cotton balls fall off the table (while you blow them off). Count the "snowflakes" as they fall to the floor. Now allow your child to blow the "snowflakes" off the table while you sit under the table and watch.

Allow your child to sit on a sled inside the house. Pull it around on the carpet (if it will not damage the floor). Teach your child opposites by allowing him to request to go "fast" or "slow".

While playing, encourage your child to do the following: 1) label the winter clothing items (hat, mitten, scarf) and 2) label the body parts they go on (i.e. hat/head, mitten/hand, and coat/body). Talk about snow characteristics. How does it feel? From where does the snow fall? Why does it disappear?

Share vs. Turn Taking

Target of This Activity

This activity is designed to teach your child to take turns with peers by encouraging positive social skills.

Materials

Toys

Friends

Example Target Words

Beginning Words	Simple Words	Difficult Words
Please Thank you	Counting 1–10 Trade	Take turns My turn Your turn

Rationale

Playing with peers or siblings is a wonderful way to work on social skills. "Sharing" is an abstract and difficult concept for young children to understand. From a young child's perspective, his toy is getting taken away with no plan of when he can get it back. In our practice as speech pathologists, we have found that using the term "turn" instead of "share" is a simple way to greatly boost a child's understanding. Taking turns is a more concrete concept which results in better behavior.

Procedure

When your child argues over toys, encourage him to "take turns" as opposed to "share". For example, when a dilemma arises, say, "Once we count to ten, it will be Henry's turn." Then count slowly to ten. Encourage your child to count with you.

Once you reach ten, give your child a chance to hand over the toy. If he refuses, help him. Then allow the second child to play with the toy for a turn. Count to ten again and switch turns.

Alternatively, introduce a second item so that the children can "trade" toys each time you count to ten. Trading allows them to take turns with different toys.

Making Choices

Target of This Activity

This activity is designed to teach your child vocabulary words. Following simple directions, making choices, and fine motor skills are also targeted in this activity.

Materials

Board puzzle

Bag

Example Target Words

Beginning Words	Simple Words	Difficult Words
Bye-bye	Pig Please Horse Cow	I want ___ Thank you Puzzle

Procedure

Work with your child on a board puzzle. We recommend starting with farm/animal puzzles or vehicle puzzles.

Making Choices: Encourage your child to make choices. Place all the puzzle pieces out of your child's view. Sit in front of your child and hold up two puzzle pieces (one in each hand). Ask your child, "Do you want the cow or the pig?" You can also use animal sounds if your child does not yet say words. For example, "Do you want the animal that says moo or neigh?" Your child may try to reach for the puzzle piece instead of verbalizing its name. Simply move it out of his reach, make eye contact, and model the name (or sound) of the desired animal for him. Encourage your child to imitate you by adding, "Now you say!"

Making Requests: Modify this activity as your child's language develops. Hold up a puzzle piece and encourage your child to request it by saying "I want" or "please".

Receptive Vocabulary: Once your child has completed the puzzle, hold out a bag and say, "Put the cow in the bag." Wait for your child to look at the pieces, find the cow, take the cow off of the puzzle board, and place it in the bag. As your child does so, encourage him to say "bye-bye, cow".

If your child picks up the dog instead of the cow, say, "That's not the cow, that's a dog! Find the cow and put it in the bag." Continue until all of the pieces are in the bag.

Up, Up, and Away!

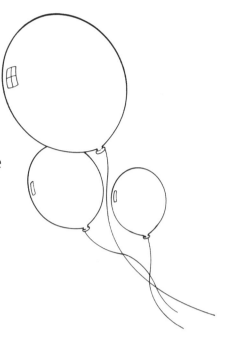

Target of This Activity

This activity is designed to encourage your child to make requests and learn to answer simple "where" questions.

Materials

Balloons*

Hand pump

Example Target Words

Beginning Words	Simple Words	Difficult Words
More	Again	Ready, set go!
Help	On top	Where is it?
Up	Balloon	There it is!
Away		Beside the couch

Procedure

Blow up a balloon with a hand pump. Stop and encourage your child to tell you "more". Allow your child to help you push the end of the pump so that air fills the balloon. See if your child can pump up the balloon by himself. Encourage your child to ask for "help". Continue to blow up the balloon.

Once it is full, stop pumping and say, "Ready, set, go!" Let go of the balloon and watch it zoom and swirl across the room. As it flies, say, "Up, up, and away!" Once it lands, say, "Where did it go?" "There it is!" Teach your child prepositions such as "on the table" (on top), or "beside the couch". Encourage your child to ask for this game "again".

*Careful! Balloons can be choking hazards and may contain latex. Recommended for ages three and up. Adult supervision required.

Treasure Hunt

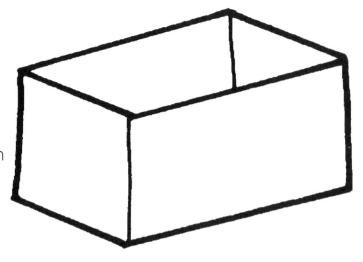

Target of This Activity

This activity is designed to teach your child to say the names of five new objects and how to play with/use each of them appropriately.

Materials

Large box

Packing peanuts*

5-7 unfamiliar objects

Example Target Words

Beginning Sounds	Simple Words	Difficult Words
Choo choo	Bubbles	Boat
Beep (car)	Baby	Book
Eee-ooo-eee-ooo	Puppy	Car
(firetruck siren)	Apple	Truck
Brrng (telephone)	Ball	Plane
	Doll	

Procedure

Many children love finding hidden objects. Place five unfamiliar objects in a box. Pour packing foam ("peanuts") on top of the objects so they are hidden.

Show your child the box. Encourage your child to reach into the box and find the hidden "treasures". As he finds an object, say the name of the object and encourage your child to do the same. Take time to play with the new toys/objects and show him how they work. Use simple words and encourage him to imitate you.

*Careful! Young children may try to eat the packing peanuts so be certain to watch your child closely. Recommended for ages 3 and up. For younger children, this activity can be modified by hiding the objects in a big duffel bag (without the packing peanuts). Allow your child to reach into the bag to find an object without peeking.

Juice Lid Game

Target of This Activity

Some children benefit from practicing the same words repeatedly in order to master the correct pronunciation. This activity is designed to encourage repetition.

Materials

Baby food jar lids

Coffee can (or other metal can with lid)

Pictures of target words

Tape

Example Target Words

Beginning Words	Simple Words	Difficult Words
Mama	Baby	Bottle
Dada	Apple	Sun
Bye-bye	Hot	Car
Hi	Boat	Tree
Boo boo (picture of bandaid)	Ball	Shake
	Moon	Put in
	Eat	Plink

Procedure

Collect ten metal baby food jar lids ("tokens"). Next, make your "token" can. To do this, make a three inch by one inch slit in the plastic lid of a coffee can. Next, place the lid on the top of the can. Drop a "token" into the can and listen. The "clink" sound you hear is very reinforcing to many children. Below are some "token" can activities.

Same Word Practice: To practice one word many times, tape a picture of the target word you would like for your child to practice onto the side of the can. Encourage your child to say the desired word. When your child attempts to say the word, say "Yeah!" and hand your child a baby food jar lid. Tell your child to "put in". Say "plop" or "plink" as the lid hits the bottom of the jar and clap your hands to encourage your child to say more words. When all the lids are in the can, let your child "shake, shake, shake" and then "dump out".

Multiple Words Practice: If you would like for your child to practice several different words, tape pictures of the target words onto the top of each baby food jar lid. Show your child the lid and encourage him to identify the picture. When your child attempts to say the desired word, say "Yeah!" and hand your child a baby food jar lid. Tell your child to "put in". Say "plop" or "plink" as the lid hits the bottom of the jar and clap your hands to encourage your child to say more words. When all the lids are in the can, let your child "shake, shake, shake" and then "dump out".

Going on a Safari

Target of This Activity

This activity is designed to teach taking turns, eye contact, verbal interaction, and -ing words. It is also designed to teach three-word phrases and basic concepts, such as quiet and loud.

Materials

Safari hat

Pictures of animals taped around house (magazine or clip art)

Flashlight

Example Target Words

Beginning Words	Simple Words	Difficult Words
Roar (lion sound) Shh Oo-oo-ee (monkey)	Eat Sit Nap Hippo	Sleeping Walking Running Jumping Drinking

Procedure

Many children love pretend play. This activity is a wonderful way to work on -ing words and three-word phrases.

Pretend you are going on a safari around your house. Put on (or make) a safari hat and quietly walk around the house looking for pretend animals with a flashlight. Walk on your tip toes. Say "shh". Encourage your child to be quiet so that animals do not get scared away.

Walk over by the couch, point the flashlight, and say, "Oh look! Do you see the hippo? What is he doing? He is sitting." Then say, "Let's see if we can find some more animals." Continue walking around the house. Stop near different areas such as the sink, refrigerator, table, or door.

See if your child can imagine different animals. Ask your child, "What do you see? What does the animal say?" Say some sounds loudly (i.e. bear-roar) and other sounds quietly (giraffe-eating leaves). Continue to work on -ing by talking about what the animal is doing (eating, sleeping, walking, running, jumping, etc.) Encourage your child to say, "He is sleeping". Also, talk about what your child is doing (walking, looking, taking pretend pictures, etc.) Encourage him to say, "I am walking."

Flash Card Steps

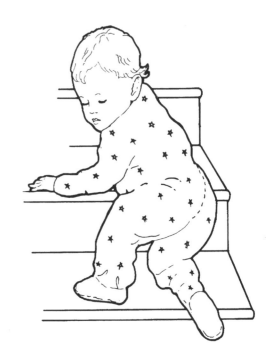

Target of This Activity

This activity is designed to teach your child to identify and say the names of various objects.

Materials

First word flash cards or clip art pictures

Empty tissue box

Example Target Words

Beginning Words	Simple Words	Difficult Words
Ball	Baby	Juice
Eat	Bottle	Car
Bye-bye	Book	Dog
Mama	Hi	Cat
Dada	Boat	

Procedure

We have listed some common first words above. Make your own first word flash cards using clip art on the computer. Alternatively, print pictures taken with your camera (dog, cat, mama, etc.). Feel free to create target words of your own.

Place the pictures around your house. Make a path around your house and follow the trail of flashcards through each room. As your child comes to a new flash card, allow him to pick it up and try to say the word. Show your child how to place it through the slit of an empty tissue box.

Do you have stairs* in your house? Place one flashcard on each step. As you walk up each step, say the name of the picture on the flashcard. Pick up the card and encourage your child to imitate you. Children love to collect and hold the cards. Placing the card in the box is also very reinforcing!

*Careful! Children must be supervised when playing on the stairs!

Treasure Hunt w/
Photos

Blanket Fort

Target of This Activity

This activity is designed to teach your child spatial concepts and action words. It also introduces your child to simple "where" questions.

Materials

Blankets

Chairs and/or tables

Example Target Words

Beginning Words	Simple Words	Difficult Words
Help	Table	Inside (fort)
Big	Fort	Outside (fort)
On	Under (table)	Beside
Out	Pig	Next to
In	Big	Blanket
	Bad	Chair
	Puff	Wolf

Procedure

Children love to climb in, under, and through things. Make a fort by draping blankets over a table and/or chairs.

Where Questions: Ask your child "where" questions while he plays in the fort. Ask, "Where are you?" Encourage him to answer using spacial prepositions such as "in", "out", "inside", "outside", "next to", and "under".

Fort Play: Once your fort is built, read a book or have a special snack inside the fort. Children are often much more vocal when they are in a special place with fewer distractions. Playing in a fort is a wonderful way to focus on your child's communication because the distractions are limited. At night it is also fun to use a flashlight in the fort to read books or make funny sounds as you flash the flashlight on and off.

Dramatic Play: Take some special toys into the fort and show your child how to pretend play. Allow your child to choose a character from a story and act out that story using the fort. For example, play *The Three Little Pigs*. While your child is inside the fort, stand outside and say, "Little pig, little pig, let me in!" Your child can say "no", or "Go away!" Tell your child, "Then I will huff and puff and blow your house in!" Gently tear the fort apart while huffing and puffing. Help your child rebuild the fort. Repeat the dialog, but this time pretend the fort is too sturdy for the wolf to blow down.

Chapter 4

Outdoor Play

Park Playground Theme

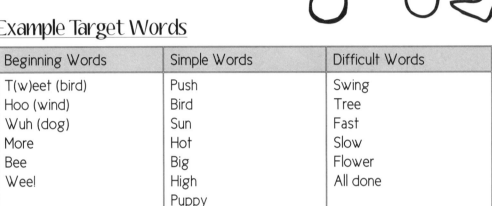

Target of This Activity

This activity is designed to encourage your child to say environmental sounds and simple words.

Materials

Playground or park

Example Target Words

Beginning Words	Simple Words	Difficult Words
T(w)eet (bird)	Push	Swing
Hoo (wind)	Bird	Tree
Wuh (dog)	Sun	Fast
More	Hot	Slow
Bee	Big	Flower
Wee!	High	All done
	Puppy	

Procedure

On the Way to the Park: Talk about what you see on the way to the park (bee, tree, ball, sun, bird). Ask, "What do you see?" Encourage your child to point and respond.

Depending on the level of your child's speech, accept approximations like "teet" for "tweet" or "mo" for "more". (These words can be "shaped" later on. For now just encourage sounds and words.) If your child is more advanced, encourage phrases like "big tree" or "hot sun".

At the Park: Use a swing or teeter totter to encourage eye contact and first words like "more", "push", "fast", "all done", and "high". Hold onto the swing or pause the teeter totter and wait for your child to request a turn by saying, "more" or "please".

Teach Commenting: Commenting in the context of language development is described as a person communicating in order to share an experience. It is not a request ("May I have that?") or demand ("Give me that").

Encourage your child to show things to you. Talk about the objects you see and the sounds you hear. Listen for the sound of birds, the wind, dogs barking, and cars passing. Listen and watch your child to see what he is trying to show you.

Once you know what he is trying to show you, model the sound ("meow" for a cat) or name of the object ("cat"). Hopefully, the next time he sees the object, he will let you know by pointing and saying "meow" or "cat".

Painting Outside

Target of This Activity

This activity is designed to teach your child to say phrases.

Materials

Paintbrush

Bucket

Bubbles (optional)

1/4 cup cornstarch

Water

Food coloring

Example Target Words

Beginning Phrases	Simple Phrases	Difficult Phrases
Dump out All gone	Water paint Where go? I paint More paint	Water go bye-bye Pretty picture I see water

Procedure

Children love playing outside. There are so many things for them to talk about and explore. Here are some suggestions for enhancing speech and language while your child is outside.

Water Painting: Fill a container with warm water. Give your child a two or three inch paintbrush. Show him how to dip the paintbrush in the water and allow him to "paint" on a brick surface or sidewalk. Watch as the "paint" evaporates in the sun! Mess-free and worry-free! Optionally, add bubbles or food coloring. Practice phrases like "dump out", "water paint", "I see water" and "all gone".

Sidewalk Paint: You'll need: 1/4 cup cornstarch, 1/4 cup water, and 6–8 drops of food coloring. Mix the cornstarch and cold water together. Add food coloring and stir. Repeat to make different colors. Encourage your child to paint pictures on the sidewalk. NOTE: This paint can be easily washed off with water and is great for painting large areas temporarily! Practice phrases like, "pretty picture", "I paint", and "more paint".

Magic Shadows

Target of This Activity

This activity is designed to teach your child to say phrases.

Materials

Construction paper

Scissors

Blocks

Cutout alphabet letters

Cutout shapes (circle, square, triangle)

Leaves

Sunny day

Example Target Words

Beginning Phrases	Simple Phrases	Difficult Phrases
On top Paper down	Sun paint Now wait We wait	Block on paper Leaf on paper

Procedure

Children love playing outside. There are so many things for them to talk about and explore. Here are some suggestions for enhancing speech and language while your child is outside.

Sun Painting: Take a dark colored piece of construction paper outside with 4-5 distinct objects (i.e. blocks, letters, shapes, scissors, leaves, etc.). Place the paper on the ground in direct sunlight. A sideway or driveway works best. Place the objects on the paper and wait. Model phrases such as "on top", "block down", "circle on top", and "leaf on top".

After two hours of "baking" in the direct sunlight, the paper will fade around the objects. Take the objects off the paper. Show your child where the sun has faded the paper. Practice words like, "ball on top", "sun paint", or "leaf on paper".

Puddles, Rain, or Night

Target of This Activity

This activity is designed to provide you with some simple ideas that will allow you to practice speech and language in a way that is exciting and new for your child.

Materials

Umbrella (optional)

Flashlight (optional)

Example Target Words

Beginning Words	Simple Words	Difficult Words
In	Rain	Over
Wet	Bird	Jump
Up	Light	Worm
High	Go!	I see ___
Moon	Day	Star
	Away	Puddle

Procedure

Puddles: Many children love playing in puddles! Go outside after it rains and find some puddles. Encourage your child to count how many puddles he can find. Jump in them or over them! Each time say, "Ready, set, go!" or "jump".

Rain Walk: Some children become more vocal in new situations because they are excited. During a light spring shower, put on your raincoats, grab the umbrella, and take a walk. Your child will likely love listening to the rain and looking for worms and birds. Talk about what you see. Model phrases like, "I see ___".

Encourage your child to say a word or two from the following poem. We recommend the following underlined words:

Rain, rain, <u>go</u> away,

Come again another <u>day</u>!

Night Walk: Use a flashlight and take your child on a night walk. Encourage your child to say "moon", "stars", and "lights". Some children love taking a walk after it snows because it is so quiet and peaceful outside. Say poems like:

Star light star bright,

First star I <u>see</u> tonight,

I wish I may I wish I might,

Have the <u>wish</u> I wish tonight.

Twinkle, twinkle little star,

How I wonder what you are.

<u>Up</u> above the world so <u>high</u>

Like a diamond in the sky.

Pool/Sprinkler Fun

Target of This Activity

This activity is designed to teach your child adjectives, action words, and spatial concepts while cooling off in the hot summer sun.

Materials

Pool or sprinkler

Cup or bucket

Example Target Words

Beginning Words	Simple Words	Difficult Words
Wee	Hose	Sprinkler
Help	Pool	Water on
Please	Cup	Water off
Water	Cold	Will you help me?
In	Turn on	Sitting
Out	Hold	Jumping
On	Big	Small

Procedure

Small (Kiddie) Pool: Ask your child to help you fill up the pool by saying, "Will you help me?" Children often want to act "grown up". Sometimes they think that grown ups do not need to ask for help. It is important for parents to model how to ask for help. Allow your child to "hold the hose" or "turn on the water".

Encourage your child to use words like, "in", "out", "brr", "cold". Have your child talk about what he is doing in the pool: sitting, standing, jumping, etc. Use a cup and put water "in" and then allow your child to dump it "out".

Sprinkler: Attach a sprinkler to your hose and encourage your child to say "water on". Leave the water on for a minute and then turn it off. Encourage your child to say "oops" or "water off". Encourage your child to make a request by asking "on" or "Water on, please!" Run through the sprinkler and say "wee" or "Ready, set, go!" Turn the sprinkler up high and down low while encouraging words such as "big" and "small".

Please note: It is never safe to leave children alone with water. Adult supervision is required.

Leaves

Target of This Activity

This activity is designed to teach your child action words, size comparisons, and simple requesting.

Materials

Leaves

Rake

Example Target Words

Beginning Words	Simple Words	Difficult Words
More	Big	Bigger
Yes	Again	More leaves
No	Fast	Ready, set, go!
Up	Slow	Bedroom
Down		Kitchen
		Garage

Procedure

These autumn activities teach your child to have fun in the fallen leaves.

Falling Leaves: For younger children, sit on the ground in the leaves and throw the leaves in the air. Watch the leaves fall down. Encourage your child to say "more", "again", "up", and "down".

Leaf Races: Walk around and find the largest leaf you can. Once both you and your child have collected a large leaf, hold the leaves horizontally about three feet up in the air. Ask, "Which leaf will fall faster? Mine or yours?" Encourage your child to respond and say, "Ready, set, go!" Repeat the activity and predict which leaf will fall more slowly.

Big & Bigger: Rake leaves into a pile in your yard. While raking, use words such as "big", "bigger", "more", and "more leaves". Stop what you are doing and ask your child, "Do we need more?" Encourage your child to respond with "yes", "no", "more" or "more leaves". After you have a large pile, have fun in the leaves! Step back and say, "Ready, set, go!" and run and jump into the pile. Next time, see if your child can fill in the blank with "Ready, set, ___".

House of Leaves: Make a house by raking the leaves into lines (like the blueprint of a house). Leave gaps for doorways. Create an entire house of leaves. Rake the leaves into large squares for the kitchen, living room, and bedroom. Add a line of leaves for the hallway. Practice labeling "bedroom", "kitchen", "bathroom", and "hallway". Quiz your child by asking, "Which room has a bed in it?" Encourage your child to answer "bedroom".

Chapter 5

Kitchen/ Mealtime

Chef Time!

Target of This Activity

This activity is designed to encourage your child to use simple words and practice turn taking while making pretend dough.

Materials

Bowls (4)

Spoons

Water

Flour

Rolling pin

Sugar

Teaspoon

Measuring cups

Food coloring (optional)

Example Target Words

Beginning Words	Simple Words	Difficult Words
Me	Please	Spoon
My	Dough	Bowl
In	Dump	Stir
Out	Cup	Roll
More	Pin	Colors
	Water	Sticky
		Dry

Procedure

Get out the bowls and spoons! Place some flour, sugar, and water in separate bowls on a table along with a large, empty bowl, measuring cups, and spoons. Tell your child, "It is time to make some pretend dough."

Show your child how to scoop flour, water, and sugar using a measuring cup. Pour each ingredient into the (empty) bowl. Do not worry about following a specific recipe. Instead, allow your child to play and have fun. Encourage him to experiment with quantities. Add water to make the dough pasty. Talk about how the dough feels "sticky", "pasty", or "dry".

Your child may want to use a spoon to stir, scoop, and dump the dough back into the bowl. Practice saying words like "dough", "dump out", "stir", "my turn", and "please". Add food coloring and practice labeling colors. Roll the dough with a rolling pin and show your child how to knead the dough using his hands. Press cookie cutters into the dough and label the shape. Throw the "dough" away when done.

Playful Picnic

Target of This Activity

This activity encourages initiation, requesting, verbalizations (environmental noises) and increases understanding (receptive vocabulary).

Materials

Blanket

Plates

Napkins

Toy food

Basket

Stuffed animals (optional)

Example Target Words

Beginning Words	Simple Words	Difficult Words
Smack lips	I do	Plate
Gulp (drinking noises)	Apple	Yours
Me/mine	Banana	Sit down
Mmm	Milk	Cup
More (sign or word)	Water	Good
Oops		Blanket

Procedure

Fun for indoors or out! Lay a blanket on the floor. Place toy food in a basket. For a bigger party, put some of your child's favorite stuffed animals on the blanket.

Sit down and begin to pass out plates and cups. "Forget" to give your child a plate or cup. Encourage him to interact by asking, "Who needs a plate?"

Next get the food out and pretend to eat it. Make smacking noises as you pretend to eat the food and gulping noises as you pretend to drink from a cup. Ask your child, "Do you want more food?" Encourage him to say "more".

Pretend to spill your milk and encourage your child to say "oops" or "uh-oh". Practice wiping your mouth with a napkin. Place the napkin in your lap. Model appropriate manners and encourage your child to do the same.

Label the food ("apple", "banana", "milk") and utensils ("bottle", "cup", "spoon"). As you clean up, ask, "May I have the cup, please?" Continue until your child has handed you all of the picnic items.

Kitchen Drawer

Target of This Activity

This pretend play activity is designed to teach your child kitchen vocabulary, simple requesting, and how to follow simple directions.

Materials

Kitchen drawer

Plastic containers with lids

Plastic cups

Plastic bowls

Example Target Words

Beginning Words	Simple Words	Difficult Words
Eat	Lid	Hungry
More	Bottle	Thirsty
In	Bowl	Spoon
Out	Cup	Stir
	Open	Drink

Procedure

The first step in this activity is to make a special place in the kitchen for your child that is his own. We recommend emptying a kitchen cabinet drawer that is close to the ground, easy to open, and out of the main cooking path/area. Your child will feel important and gain independence when he has his own kitchen space.

Fill the drawer with various plastic containers, cups, lids, and plastic bowls. Tell your child, "This is your drawer." If your child likes to open all the other drawers in the kitchen, explain, "That is Mommy's drawer. Your drawer is over here". Show your child his drawer. Continue to redirect your child to his drawer whenever necessary.

If your child is not yet using words, encourage him to independently get a bowl or cup when he is hungry or thirsty and bring it to you. This teaches him to make eye contact, gain attention, interact, and make requests. Once he is consistently handing you empty bowls and cups to request food and drinks, encourage him to verbalize as he hands you the bowl by saying "more" or "eat".

Chapter 6

Night Time Routine

Bath Tub Party

Target of This Activity

This activity is designed to teach your child how to say specific sounds and words while taking a bath. Promoting speech and language development during bath time is important because the child is attentive to the caregiver and bath time happens routinely.

Materials

Foam pictures, letters, or numbers

Shaving cream

Example Target Words:

Beginning Words	Simple Words	Difficult Words
More	Push	A, B, C... (Letters)
Yeah	Help	1, 2, 3... (Numbers)
Up	Down	
Ball	Apple	
Me	Please	

Procedure

Squeeze some shaving cream onto your child's hand and show him how to rub the shaving cream on the bottom of the foam pictures or letters. Alternatively, you can also put the shaving cream on each picture and hand it to your child. Show your child how to 'push' them onto the tub wall. Watch them stick to the wall! Name the pictures and practice saying words like 'push', 'help', 'more please', and 'yeah'. After all the pictures are up, ask your child to take them down (or knock them down). Work on comprehension by asking your child, 'Can you knock down the black and white animal?' Further, you could say, 'Give daddy the cow' or 'Give daddy the letter 'c''.

Other Ideas:

- Focus on themes or categories – animals, vehicles, etc. For example, ask your child to put all the animals on one side of the bath tub and the vehicles on the other side.

- Focus on colors or patterns. Ask your child to group the pictures or letters by color or picture pattern (wavy line, polka dots, etc.).

Please Note: Never leave a child unattended while taking a bath. Adult supervision required at all times!

Books, Books, Books!

Target of This Activity

This activity is designed to teach parents language enriching activities that can be implemented during story time.

Materials

Books (see recommended books below)

Procedure

Here are some storybook techniques that can help encourage both speech and language development.

Sounds Only: Occasionally conduct story time without reading any of the words in the book! Take a storybook and focus only on the sounds that can be associated with the pictures. Model the corresponding sounds as you point to the pictures. Encourage your child to say the sounds and point to the pictures. Some examples are:

1. A picture of a firehouse with a fire pole – "wee" (use your index finger and slide it from the top to the bottom of the fire pole)
2. A Dalmatian dog – "woof woof" says the dog
3. A phone on the table – "ring ring" (point to the phone)
4. A siren/bell on the wall – "clang clang" goes the bell
5. A bee flying over the flowers in the window – "bzz" (point to the bee)

Rhythmic Books: Look for repetitious, melodic books like *Brown Bear, Brown Bear* (by B. Martin and E. Carle). Choose one or two simple words from the story and encourage your child to imitate them. For example, in *Brown Bear, Brown Bear* encourage your child to say "you" and/or "see". If your child cannot yet say these words, encourage gestures (pointing to eyes) so that he can participate, respond, and interact with you.

Below is a list of some rhythmic books that will help get you started. The target words we recommend are in quotes.

1. *Here Are My Hands* by Martin and Archambault: "my" or body parts
2. *How Do Dinosaurs Play with Their Friends?* by Yolen and Teague (entire series): "he"
3. *Ten Little Ladybugs* by Gerth and Huliska-Beith: "bugs"

Repetitive Word Books: Look for books that have a simple word repeated throughout the book like C. Schneider's *Who Stole the Cookie from the Cookie Jar?* In this example, encourage your child to say "me" or "who". While reading, point to your child and then pause when it is his turn to say the word. Each time you come across that word in the story, point to your child and encourage him to say it.

Below is a list of some repetitive books that will help get you started. The target words we recommend are in quotes.

1. *That's Not My Puppy...* by F. Watt (entire series): "puppy"

2. *How Kind!* by M. Murphy: "How Kind!"

3. *I'll Teach My Dog a Lot of Words* by M. Frith: "teach" or "him"

Books for Comprehension

Target of This Activity

This activity is designed to teach your child beginning comprehension skills. It will familiarize your child with wh- questions and sentence structure.

Materials:

Book: *Goldilocks and the Three Bears* (by various authors)

Procedure

Sometimes parents get so focused on encouraging their late talker to express himself through words that they forget it is also important to focus on receptive language. Receptive language is what your child understands. Here are some simple activities that you can implement in your daily reading routine that will target receptive language.

Ask Questions: Picture books have nice illustrations that are perfect for asking your child specific questions about the content of the story. Ask questions about the pictures to help ensure his understanding.

Start with simple questions (3-4 words in length) that your child can answer by simply pointing to pictures. For example, in *Goldilocks and the Three Bears*, start with beginning comprehension questions such as, "Where is the table?", "Where is the bowl?", "Who is eating?", "Who is walking?", "Who ate the food?", and "Who broke the chair?" These questions can be answered by simply pointing to the pictures.

As your child correctly answers these questions, slowly start to elicit more information from your child. For example:

1.   Q: "Who eats from the big bowl?" A: "Papa Bear."

2.   Q: "Are the three bears happy when they come home?" A: "No."

3.   Q: "How do they feel?" A: "Sad."

Gradually build up the level of difficulty of each question. This will enhance story time for your child and will improve his understanding of the book.

Memory: After you finish a story, turn back to the beginning of the book. Ask your child, "What happened first?" or "Now it's your turn to tell me the story!" Allow your child to look at the picture to get ideas. See if your child can tell you the main parts of the story.

What Would You Do? See if your child can role play himself into the story. What would your child do if he was Goldilocks and the three bears came home? What would your child do if he was the baby bear? The momma bear? The daddy bear?

New Endings: Ask your child if he liked the ending of the book. Tell your child how you would change the ending of the story. Make it silly or sad. Now ask your child how he would change the ending of the story.

Toothbrush Talk

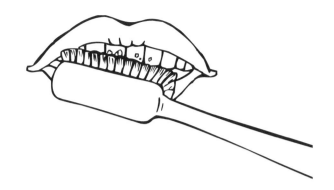

Target of This Activity

This activity is designed to stimulate your child's oral musculature in preparation for speech.

Materials

Vibrating toothbrush

Mirror (optional)

Rationale

A vibrating toothbrush used daily can stimulate the muscles used for speech. Use it not only to brush your child's teeth, but also to "wake up" the inside of their mouths – namely, cheeks, gums, and tongue. Some children don't realize all the muscles they have control of for speech until they have been "worked out". This exercise provides sensation to the oral musculature, which in turn, helps your child become more aware of their mouth and the muscles inside it. Be careful not to put the toothbrush too far back in the child's mouth. Also, it is important to note that some children may resist the following exercises because of sensory defensiveness. Consult a speech therapist for more information.

Procedure

Inside Cheek Rub: Rub a vibrating toothbrush gently over the inside of your child's cheeks for five seconds on each side of his mouth. Gently move the toothbrush in circles trying to stimulate the inside surface of his cheeks.

Tongue Rub: Ask your child to stick out his tongue and gently stroke the vibrating toothbrush down the center of the tongue. Start a third of the way back and pull out toward the tip of the tongue. Repeat five times. If your child is hesitant to try this exercise, start with the toothbrush turned off until your child feels more comfortable with this sensation. Next, stroke each side of the tongue. Use the vibrating toothbrush to gently stroke the right and left edges of the tongue. Once again, start in the back of the mouth and gently stroke the vibrating toothbrush over the tongue, pulling out toward the front of the mouth.

Outside Cheek Rub: Turn the toothbrush over and massage the outer cheeks with the flat side of the toothbrush while the toothbrush is turned on. Rest the toothbrush on your child's cheek and gently rub the outside of your child's cheek. Once again, start with the toothbrush in the back (near the ear) and pull forward toward the corner of the lips. Lift up the toothbrush and repeat five times on each side of the face.

Toothbrush Talk: Ask your child, "What does your toothbrush sound like?" Encourage your child to make the toothbrush sound by rolling the /b/ sound off his lips over and over again (like raspberries).

Finger Play

Target of This Activity

This activity is designed to teach your child imitation and anticipation. Finger plays encourage language development, eye contact, and social play.

Example Target Words

Beginning Words	Simple Words	Difficult Words
Bed	Turtle	Sleeps
Down	Puddle	Morning
Head	Bees	Mosquito
Up		Beehive
Me		
Bzz (bee)		

Procedure

The finger plays below are perfect for daily bedtime routines. Over time your child may begin to say some of the words or do the gestures with you! Encourage your child to say the underlined words below.

Going to Bed:

This little boy is going to <u>bed</u> (place right forefinger in left hand)

<u>Down</u> on the pillow he lays his <u>head</u>,

Wraps himself in the cover tight (fold left hand over right forefinger)

This is the way he sleeps all night,

Morning comes and he opens his eyes (blink eyes as if just opening)

Back with a toss the cover flies,

<u>Up</u> he jumps, is dressed, and away

Ready for work, ready for play (Open left fist and quickly raise right forefinger, then wiggle it and move hand as if walking on its way.)

There Was a Little Turtle:

There was a little <u>turtle</u>, (make a small circle w/hand)

He lived in a box, (make box w/hand)

He swam in a <u>puddle</u> (wiggle hands)

He climbed on the rock. (stack hands on the other)

He snapped at a mosquito, (clap hands)

He snapped at a flea, (clap hands)

He snapped at a minnow, (clap hands)

He snapped at <u>me</u> (clap hands)

He caught the mosquito, (clap hands)

He caught the flea, (clap hands)

He caught the minnow, (clap hands)

But he didn't catch <u>me</u>! (shake index finger)

Beehive:

Here is a beehive. (make a large circle w/ both hands)

Where are all the <u>bees</u>? (gesture 'where' with hands)

Hidden away where nobody sees! (put hand above eyes as if looking in the distance)

Open it up and out they fly (pull hands apart to open the hive)

One! Two! Three! Four! Five! <u>Bzz</u>! (count with your fingers)

Chapter 7

Craft Time

Encouraging communication during craft time is an excellent way to practice speech and language. For other simple craft ideas, visit our website at www.TalkingChild.com.

Please Note: Do not leave child unattended during crafts.

Big Box Fun

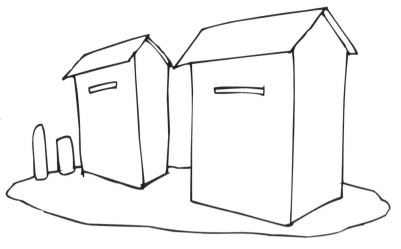

Target of This Activity

This activity is designed to teach your child beginning sounds and words while building his imagination and increasing his desire to communicate.

Materials

Box

Crayons

Example Target Words

Beginning Words	Simple Words	Difficult Words
Toot (car)	Dirty	Dry
Neigh (horse)	Wet	Clean
Open	Dry	Who's there?
In	Clip clop	Creak
Out	Yee-hah!	Castle
Bzz (bee)	House	All-aboard!
Down	Door	Chugga chugga
Mmm (flower smells good)	Ding Dong	Knock
		Stop
		Train

Procedure

Find a big cardboard box and color it to make a creative scene such as a car wash, castle, house, boxcar train, or train tunnel.

Car Wash: Turn a large box over and cut out part of it to make a tunnel. Practice words associated with a car wash like "toot", "wet", "dry", "dirty", and "clean". Send a toy car through the wash. Did the car get clean? If your box is big enough, your child can pretend to be the dirty car and go through the car wash, too.

Castle: Find a large box and draw a stone wall and/or windows on it. Add a piece of cloth to the top as a flag. Pretend to ride a horse on your way to the castle ("clip clop, clip clop", "yee-hah"); or lower the rusty drawbridge ("down", "creak"); or knock on the castle door ("knock", "ding dong", "Who's there?").

House: Draw a big house on a cardboard box. Make a front door and windows. Add flowerboxes and bees under the windows. Practice words associated with a house: "door", "open", "in", "out", "mmm" (good smelling flower), and "bzz".

Train: Attach several shoe boxes together and make a boxcar train. Practice words like "All-aboard!", "choo choo", and "chugga chugga". Alternatively, use one big box to make a train tunnel. Watch your toy train go through the tunnel.

Gone Fishing

Target of This Activity

This activity is designed to encourage your child to say simple words, use some two-word phrases, and learn basic concepts like same and different.

Materials

Step One
- Paper
- Crayons
- Scissors
- Metal paper clips

Step Two
- String
- Stick
- Magnet
- Fish from step one

Example Target Words

Beginning Words	Simple Words	Difficult Words
Ball	Big	Big fish
Boat	Fish	Catch fish
Bee	Please	No match
Bubble	Same	Different
Baby		My turn
Bird		Your turn

Procedure

This activity can be done in two steps.

Step One: Use paper and crayons to make fish of different sizes, shapes, and colors. Focus on concepts like "big", "fish", "big fish", "little fish", "blue fish", "two fish", and "my fish". Cut out the fish. Next, draw some simple pictures on the back of each fish (ex. ball, boat, bee, baby, bottle, bird, dog, bubble, or book). Alternatively, print clip art pictures and tape them to the back of each fish. Finally, attach a metal paperclip to each fish. Now you are ready to play the game described in Step Two.

Step Two: Spread the fish out on the floor so the picture is facing down. Make a fishing pole by tying a string to the end of a stick. Then, tie a small magnet to the end of the string. Hold the fishing pole over the fish until your magnet attracts a paperclip (attached to a fish). Pull up the fishing pole so that the fish is off the ground. Remove the fish from the magnet and say the name of the object on the back of the card. Expand your speech by adding to it—"fish", "big fish", "big red fish!"

To make the game more challenging, make two pictures of each object and tape them to the back of two separate fish. Talk about the definitions of "same and different". Each player catches two fish during his turn to see if he can make a match. If the pictures match, you may keep the fish. If not, throw them back and it is the next player's turn.

Say a Sound

Target of This Activity

This activity is designed to encourage your child to say a specific target sound several times in a row.

Materials

Construction paper

Scissors

Glue (or frosting)

Items (see example target sounds below)

Example Target Sounds

Beginning Sounds	Simple Sounds	Difficult Sounds
/p/ (popcorn) /b/ (buttons) /m/ (marshmallows)	/t/ (toothpicks) /d/ (Dots™ – gummy candy) /n/ (noodle) /w/ (water/watercolor paint) /h/ (stickers or pictures of hats)	/k/ (kites – paper diamonds) /g/ (grapes – small cutout circles) /f/ (flower stickers) /y/ (yarn pieces)

Procedure

Choose a sound to focus on with your child. Some common early developing sounds are /p, b, m, t, d, n, h, w/. Draw a large letter of the corresponding target sound on a piece of construction paper and cut it out.

For example, if working on the /m/ sound, draw a large "m" on construction paper and cut it out. Decorate the letter with items that begin with that sound. For example, decorate the "m" with marshmallows. Dip a miniature marshmallow in some cake frosting and stick it on the construction paper letter. Each time you add a new marshmallow say the sound of the letter – /m/ ("mmm").

Continue until your child has practiced the target sound 15–20 times and the construction paper is decorated. Ideas for decorating your target letter are listed above next to each sound. The sounds listed above are generally developed by age 3 ½. For a complete list of sound development, please visit www.TalkingChild.com.

Bird Seed Picture

Target of This Activity

This activity is designed to teach your child new words and simple shapes.

Materials

Construction paper

Liquid glue

Bird seed

Example Target Words

Beginning Words	Simple Words	Difficult Words
T(w)eet (bird)	Seed	Glue
Help	Bird	Bird house
More	House	Triangle
Paper	On top	Square
		Circle

Procedure

Make a bird house out of construction paper, bird seed, and glue.

First make the base of the bird house. Help your child drizzle some glue in the shape of a large square near the bottom of a piece of construction paper. Practice words like "glue", "big square", "big", and "house".

Next make the roof of the birdhouse. Make a triangle (for the roof) using the top side of the square to complete your bird house. Say words like "roof", "triangle", "on top". Finally make a small circle inside the square for the bird entrance. Practice words like "bird", "in", "out", "circle", "t(w)eet t(w)eet".

Sprinkle the bird seed on the paper so that it is on top of the glue. Let the glue dry for a few minutes before tipping the paper to remove the extra bird seed. Compliment your child on the bird house he made! Finally, work on knowledge of simple shapes by saying, "Show me the (circle)".

Handprint Flowers

Target of This Activity

This activity is designed to teach your child parts of the hand and fine motor skills. It is also beneficial for word practice.

Materials

Colored paper

Pencil

Scissors

Green pipe cleaners or straws

Tape

Stapler

Example Target Words

Beginning Words	Simple Words	Difficult Words
Hand	More tape	Finger
Tape	Leaves	Straw
Help	Pinky	Staple
Bud	Paper	Flower
	Cut	Thumb

Procedure

Ask your child to place his hand flat on a piece of paper. Use a pencil to trace around his hand. Talk about the different parts of the hand with your child as you trace around his hand. See if your child can name "thumb", "finger", "pinky", and "hand".

Next, cut out the traced hand. Individually curl each of the paper fingers around a pencil. Using the palm of the handprint, form a cone (with fingers curling outwards). Tape the cone together. The curled hand should now look similar to the bud of the flower.

As you are working with your child, use words such as "flower", "paper", "more", and "tape". Encourage your child to ask you for "help". Staple the flower bud to a pipe cleaner or a drinking straw. Draw some leaves and cut them out. Staple or tape the leaves to the straw. Make a few different flowers and put them in a vase.

Snowman

Target of This Activity

This activity is designed to encourage your child to say five to ten words during a snowman craft project.

Materials

Paper

Glue

Scissors

Cups (small, medium, and large)

Markers

Example Target Words

Beginning Words	Simple Words	Difficult Words
Dot	Hat	Big, bigger, biggest
Ball	Button	Circle
Eyes	On top	Mouth
Nose	Arm	Cut
More	Tiny	Cup

Procedure

First, make a snowman out of white paper. Trace the bottom of three different sized cups on white paper. Cut out the "snowballs". Practice words like "more", "white", "cut", "circle", "on top", "big", "bigger" and biggest" as your child is working.

Next, help your child glue each ball on a piece of paper to make a snowman. Say "dot, dot, dot" as you put little glue dots on the paper. Optionally, hold onto the glue (or markers) and have your child ask for the item ("glue, please"). Say "ball" as you push the snowballs onto the glue. Finally, use markers to draw "hat", "eyes", "nose", "arms" and "buttons" on the snowman as your child practices saying the words.

Leaf Print Crown

Target of This Activity

This activity is designed to motivate your child to take a walk outside and enjoy autumn while learning colors, size descriptions, and identifying objects.

Materials

Basket for collecting leaves

Paper

Different types of leaves

Crayons

Tape

Example Target Words

Beginning Words	Simple Words	Difficult Words
Wee!	Down	Fall down
Ta-da!	Up high	We did it!
More	Tape	Leaf in
In	Tiny	Big leaf
Out	Leaf	Little leaf
	Colors (blue, red, yellow, purple, green)	More leaves

Procedure

This craft can be divided into three segments.

Take a Walk: Go outside and collect leaves with your child. Throw some leaves up in the air and encourage your child to say "Wee!", "down", and "fall down". Collect leaves of different sizes and shapes. Practice words like "in", "up high", "big", "tiny", and "more leaves". Encourage your child to place the leaves in the basket.

Leaf Print: Once inside, put some paper flat on the table and then put a leaf under the paper. Next, use the flat side of a crayon to color (shade) the paper. Be sure to color the area where the leaf is hiding under the paper. You should begin to see the outline of the leaf as you color the paper. Encourage your child to say, "Ta-da!", "leaf", "paper", "did it", and "We did it!" Encourage your child to ask for specific crayon colors and "more" leaves.

Crown: Cut paper into a rectangular strip about three inches wide and long enough to fit around your child's forehead. Next, cut out the leaf prints and tape them to the rectangular piece of paper. Allow your child to help tape the leaves to the crown. Encourage your child to say "tape" and "push" each time he pushes the tape down onto the paper.

Paper Circles

Target of This Activity

This activity is designed to encourage your child to vocalize and imitate.

Materials

Construction paper of various colors

Scissors

Tape

Example Target Words

Beginning Words	Simple Words	Difficult Words
Vowel sounds	Papa	Dog
/p/ – "p" sound	Mama	Cat
/b/ – "b" sound	Dada	Truck
/m/ – "m" sound	Baby	Car
/t/ – "t" sound	Puppy	Cracker
/d/ – "d" sound	Ta-da!	Milk
	Uh-oh!	Juice

Procedure

Make a speech chain with your child! Cut out strips of paper about 8 inches by 1 inch. Make a circle with the strip of paper and tape it in place. Say a sound or word and encourage your child to imitate you. Use the Example Target Words above as a starting point and remember to start at his level! If your child is saying a few sounds or words, begin with a sound or word that he can already say. Encourage him to imitate you. Once he imitates the sound or word, add a ring to the first paper circle.

Continue making sounds or words and encourage your child to continue to imitate you. Work on the same sound or word for the entire chain or come up with different sounds and words. Keep adding paper circles to the chain. Make necklaces, hang them in doorways, or string them across the room. Decorate the entire house with the paper chain. Show the chain to other family members as a visual way of reinforcing all the "good talking" your child did today (or this week)!

Messy Play: Goop

Target of This Activity

This activity is designed to encourage your child to touch and experience different textures. It also teaches vocabulary, adjectives, action words, and requesting.

Materials

2 cups cornstarch

1/2 cup water

Eye dropper

Colored water (red, blue, yellow, and green food coloring)

Spoon

Popsicle sticks

Example Target Words

Beginning Words	Simple Words	Difficult Words
Uh-oh (when turns to liquid) More Help Whoa Mix	Hard Soft Water On top	Stir Spoon Stick Colors

Procedure

Mix cornstarch and water in a bowl to form a soupy mixture. Stir well (this will take some time). Encourage your child to label action words such as "mix" and "stir".

The Goop mixture is a solid, but when you touch it, it becomes a liquid! Use an eye dropper to squirt colored water on top. Encourage your child to vocalize words such as "whoa", "on top", "uh-oh", and "water".

Watch patterns emerge and colors blend together. Encourage your child to request "red, please". If your child does not want to touch the mixture, use spoons or popsicle sticks to blend. When done, use water to easily clean up the Goop.

Messy Play: Glurch

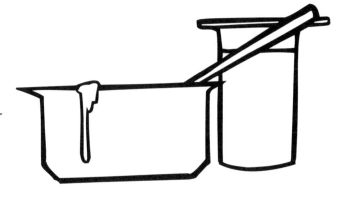

Target of This Activity

This activity is designed to encourage your child to touch and experience different textures. It also teaches vocabulary, adjectives, action words, and requesting.

Materials

2 cups white liquid glue

Water

Borax® soap

Plastic bag

Scissors (optional)

Markers (optional)

Plastic animals (optional)

Example Target Words

Beginning Words	Simple Words	Difficult Words
Open	Roll	Squeeze
Out	Bag	Stretch
More	Cut	Scissors
Help	Cow	Glue
Animal sounds (i.e. baa,	Pig	Colors
moo, neigh)	Horse	Sheep

Procedure

Mix white liquid glue with 1 ½ cups of water. Stir thoroughly. In another bowl, mix 1/3 cup water and 2 tsp. Borax® soap. Pour the Borax® mixture into the glue mixture and stir. Using your fingers, pull out the Glurch as it coagulates. Mix another solution of water and Borax® and pour into the remaining glue mixture. Stir and pull out. Continue until the glue mixture is gone.

Put mixture on wax paper. Encourage your child to use words such as those listed above by describing the Glurch, and requesting items ("scissors", "glue").

Experiment with the Glurch! Squeeze it, roll it, cut it with scissors, and color it with markers. Encourage verbalizations like "cow", "pig", "sheep", and "horse" as you drape the Glurch over the plastic animals. Watch as the Glurch takes the shape of the animals. When done, store Glurch in a plastic bag.

Messy Play: Homemade Play Dough

Target of This Activity

This activity is designed to encourage your child to touch and experiment with a different texture as well as teach vocabulary, adjectives, action words, and requesting.

Materials

Flour

Boiling water

Cream of tartar

Salt

Oil

Food coloring

Example Target Words

Beginning Words	Simple Words	Difficult Words
Open More Out Ball Help	Roll Pat, pat, pat /s/ (snake sound) Hole	Stretch Colors Pancake Snake

Procedure

This homemade play dough is not sticky and does not dry out! Combine 1 cup flour, 1 cup boiling water, 2 tbsp. cream of tartar, 1/2 cup salt, 1 tbsp. oil, and food coloring. Mix and knead together.

Homemade play dough is fun and a great activity for working on first words and sounds. Practice saying "roll" and "ball" as you roll the play dough into a ball. Encourage your child by saying, "Ball! You made a ball."

Next, show your child how to "pat, pat, pat" the ball to make the dough flat like a pancake. Now you can take the pancake and roll it into a snake. The snake says "sss".

Make some other animals to go along with your snake or make a fence, rock, grass, and water for the snake. Some snakes live in holes in the ground. Make a little hole for the snake. Each time your child uses the homemade play dough, think of a different animal to make and talk about. Teach your child vocabulary by making the animal's habitat out of play dough (i.e. where it lives, what it eats, etc.). Store play dough in an airtight bag or container in the refrigerator.

Messy Play: Ice Sculptures

Target of This Activity

This activity is designed to teach your child beginning words while exposing him to different sensory stimuli such as cold or wet objects.

Materials

Water

Containers of various shapes and sizes

Salt

Food coloring (optional)

Plastic figurines (optional)

Example Target Words

Beginning Words	Simple Words	Difficult Words
More	High	Tower
Up	Ice	Castle
Help	Water	Cold
Uh-oh	Wall	Igloo
	On top	Colors
	House	

Procedure

Freeze water in containers of various shapes and sizes (ice cube trays, popsicle trays, and plastic containers). Color the water first if you wish.

Once the water turns to ice, remove it from the containers and place it on the table. Take one piece of ice and put it on a cookie sheet. Drop spoonfuls of table salt onto the ice block. The salt acts like glue. Now add another block on top. Repeat to form ice castles or other creations.

Talk about what you are making and encourage your child to use some of the words listed above. Use words such as "igloo", "bridge", "wall", "castle", "cave", or "house". Use plastic figurines and encourage pretend play.

Some children like to re-enact their favorite fairy tales such as *The Three Little Pigs, Humpty Dumpty,* or *The Three Billy Goats Gruff* with their figurines and the ice. Talk about the cold ice. What happens to it as it melts? This activity is especially fun on a hot day!

Messy Play: Frozen Paint

Target of This Activity

This activity is designed to provide a motivating and unique activity for your child while he learns new words.

Materials

Tempera paint

Paper cups and /or ice cube trays

Foil

Popsicle sticks

Paper or cardboard

Water (optional)

Food coloring (optional)

Example Target Words

Beginning Words	Simple Words	Difficult Words
Paint Ice Name items being painted (i.e. boat, mom, baby)	Name items being painted (i.e. house, bird, sun, plane, me) Water Wet	Melt Colors Cup Cold

Procedure

This activity is recommended for outside play on a hot day. It is easy to prepare and requires little clean up. Pour paint (or equal parts of paint and water) into ice cube trays or small paper cups. (You can also freeze colored water instead of paint.) Cover the container tops with foil and insert popsicle sticks. Place in the freezer for a few hours.

Once frozen, remove the frozen paint from the container. Show your child how to hold the popsicle stick to "paint" on a variety of surfaces (paper, cardboard etc.). Talk about how the paint feels ("cold" and "wet"). Watch the frozen paint begin to melt.

Children love painting in this new way. This activity is also beneficial for encouraging communication because your child is sitting still and focused while painting. Talk about the pictures your child is painting. Make a blue sky with birds flying, a plane, and the sun. Alternatively, paint a picture of a boat sailing on water. Model words like "bird", "sun", "boat", and "water" for your child. When done, the frozen paint cleans up easily with water.

Chapter 8

Car/Travel

Sing a Song

Target of This Activity

This activity is designed to teach your child one or two simple words from the song, *Wheels on the Bus*. It is also designed to teach your child the hand movements that go along with the song. This activity encourages interaction, eye contact, and gross motor movements.

Materials

Toy bus (Optional)

Example Target Words

Beginning Words	Simple Words	Difficult Words
Beep	Baby	Bus
Wah, wah, wah	Mommy	Shut
Up	Down	Wheels
	Open	Sh, sh, sh
	Door	Move on (back)

Procedure

Children love music. Singing in the car is a wonderful way to encourage new words through music. *Wheels on the Bus* is an all-time children's favorite because it has fun, repetitive words and motions.

Sing the song slowly with deliberate hand gestures that correspond to the lyrics. If you are not familiar with the song, add your own gestures to match the lyrics of the song. Encourage your child to participate by using the hand gestures as well.

The underlined words are target words for your child to say. We have targeted them because they are simple first words and they are repeated throughout the song. Sing the song until you reach the underlined word and encourage your child to say it. Sing the target word then look at your child and say, "You say it.... BUS." Pause and wait a few seconds for a response. Praise him if he responds and continue singing the song. If he does not respond after a few seconds, continue singing and try again the next time the word "bus" is sung in the song.

> *Wheels on the Bus*
> The wheels on the <u>bus</u> go round and round,
> Round and round, round and round,
> The wheels on the <u>bus</u> go round and round,
> All through the town.

Additional verses:
The horn on the <u>bus</u> goes <u>beep, beep, beep</u>...
The door on the <u>bus</u> goes <u>open</u> and shut...
The people on the <u>bus</u> go <u>up</u> and <u>down</u>...
The baby on the <u>bus</u> goes "<u>wah, wah, wah</u>"...
The mommy on the <u>bus</u> goes "<u>sh, sh, sh</u> "...
The wipers on the <u>bus</u> go <u>swish, swish, swish</u>...
The driver on the <u>bus</u> goes "<u>move</u> on <u>back</u>"...
Author Unknown

Other Ideas:
Choose different songs or nursery rhymes to sing. Remember to add your own hand gestures to match the lyrics of the song. Here are some suggestions:

Hickory Dickory Dock
Hickory Dickory Dock
The mouse ran <u>up</u> the clock
The clock struck <u>one</u> the mouse ran <u>down</u>
Hickory Dickory Dock

Twinkle, Twinkle Little Star
Twinkle, twinkle little star
How I wonder what you are
<u>Up</u> above the world so <u>high</u>
Like a diamond in the sky
Twinkle, twinkle little star
How I wonder what <u>you</u> are

Great Big Spider (Deep Voice)
The great big spider
Went <u>up</u> the water spout
<u>Down</u> came the rain and
Washed the spider <u>out</u>
Out came the <u>sun</u> and
Dried <u>up</u> all the rain and
The great big spider went <u>up</u> the spout again

Row, Row, Row Your Boat
Row, row, row your <u>boat</u>
Gently <u>down</u> the stream
Merrily, merrily, merrily
Life is but a dream.
Row, row, row your <u>boat</u>
Gently <u>down</u> the stream
And if you see an alligator,
Don't forget to scream – <u>Ahh!</u>

Car Speech

Target of This Activity

This activity is designed to teach your child new words while driving in the car

Materials

Flashcard deck (of "first word" pictures)

Example Target Words

Beginning Words	Simple Words	Difficult Words
Ball	Dog	Light
Moon	Cat	Tree
Animal sounds	Bird	Bread
Apple	Milk	Ice cream
Bubble	Cookies	Juice
	Bubble bop	

Procedure

Practicing sounds and words in the car is a wonderful way to boost speech and language skills during your child's normal routine.

Match It: Keep flash cards in the car and/or diaper bag. (Example pictures/target words are listed above.) Ask your child to choose one card, such as a picture of a duck. Now encourage him to match the picture on the card to the real life object outside the window of the car. Say, "Can you find a duck outside?" Once your child finds a duck, choose another card (ex. "bird", "sun", "house", "dog", "ball", or "moon") and continue the matching game. Pay attention! Sometimes you can find matching pictures on billboards, too (ex. ice cream).

Animal Sounds: Look for animals outside the car window. Once your child finds an animal, say the name of the animal and the sound it makes (i.e. "cow"—"moo", "horse"—"neigh", and "cat"—"meow"). Have a contest to see which person in the car can find the most animals.

Bubble Bop: Choose a specific color of a car (ex. red) that your child can look for as you drive. Have your child say "bubble bop" each time a red car is spotted. This is an excellent way to practice the same target word multiple times. Our target word in this example is "bubble". Parents may choose any target word they would like for their child to practice and then simply add "bop" to the end.

Grocery Store

Target of This Activity

This activity is designed to teach your child colors and beginning categorization. It is also designed to teach your child how to label simple objects.

Example Target Words

Beginning Words	Simple Words	Difficult Words
Uh-oh	Apple	Carrots
Boo boo	Ba(nana)	Oranges
Bump	Beans	Grapes
Beep	Milk	Cracker
	Got it!	Cheese
	One, two...	
	Money	

Procedure

Here are some ideas for working on speech and language at the grocery store.

Involve Your Child: Involve your child in the shopping experience. In the fruit and vegetable aisle, ask him to help you choose the best apples or darkest avocados. If you see an apple that has a brown spot, you can talk about how the apple has a "boo boo" or "bump".

Counting: Ask your child to help you count as you put the apples in the bag.

Share Your List: Turn a trip to the grocery store into a scavenger hunt. Bring pictures of the healthy foods you're planning to buy. Ask your child to help you find the items by pointing or using words ("Got it!", "See it!", or "milk"). While in the produce section of the grocery store, encourage him to say the color of each selected item.

Sensory Input: Take advantage of sensory experiences. Let your child feel, smell, and even sample (where acceptable) the items you are putting in the cart.

Teach Attributes: Talk about attributes such as soft, smooth, bumpy, shiny, and firm. Help your child decide which foods fit into each category. Alternatively, see if he can categorize the foods by color. Allow him to pick out one new red (or green or orange) item to try out at home. This is a good way to get him interested in eating a variety of healthy foods.

Checking Out: When checking out, put lighter items next to your child and let him help you put them on the conveyor. Encourage beginning words like "beep" (the sound the machine makes as an item is scanned). Finally, give him some money and allow him to pay for an item of his choice.

Common First Words

apple	done	no
baa baa (sheep)	door	on
baby	down	on top
balloon	drink	open
(ba)nana	duck	owie (ouch)
bath	ear	out
bear	eat	papa
bed	eyes	piggy
bee	hair	plane
beep	hat	please
bird	help	potty
boo boo	in	pop
book	mama	puppy
boom	me	shh (quiet)
bottle	meow (cat)	shoe
bubble	milk	sock
bus	mine	toe
bye-bye	mmm (yummy)	tree
bzzz (bee)	mommy	truck
car	moo moo (cow)	tummy/belly
cheese	moon	uh-oh
choo choo	more	up
clean up	mouth	water
cookie	nap	wee
daddy	nose	wuh wuh (dog)
dog	neigh neigh (horse)	yummy
doll	nigh(t) nigh(t)	

About the Authors

Cory Poland, M.A. CCC–SLP

Cory is a mom and pediatric speech-language pathologist. She received her undergraduate degree from Purdue University and her graduate degree in communication disorders from the University of Minnesota. Cory completed her master's project on the best way to promote collaboration between speech-language pathologists and teachers in the classroom. In her practice, she has specialized in therapy for children from birth to five years of age.

Amy Chouinard, M.A. CCC–SLP

Amy is a mom and pediatric speech-language pathologist. She received her undergraduate degree in speech pathology at Marquette University and her graduate degree in communication disorders from the University of Minnesota. She completed her master's thesis on the importance of maternal-child interaction. Amy also owns a private speech therapy practice in Minneapolis, Minnesota.

References

Baxendale, J. & Hesketh, A. (2003). Comparison of the effectiveness of the Hanen Parent Programme and traditional clinic therapy. International Journal of Language and Communication Disorders, 38, 397–415.

Fey, M. E., Cleave, P. L., Long, S. H. & Hughes, D. L. (1993). Two approaches to the facilitation of grammar in children with language impairment: An experimental evaluation. Journal of Speech and Hearing Research, 36, 141–157.

Greenspan, S., & Wieder, S. (1998). The child with special needs: Encouraging intellectual and emotional growth. Reading, MA: Perseus Books.

Pianta, R. (2004). Relationships among children and adults and family literacy. In B. Wasik (Ed.), Handbook of family literacy (pp. 175–192). Mahwah, NJ: Lawrence Erlbaum.

Rosetti, L. (1990). The Rosetti infant–toddler language scale. East Moline, IL: Linguisystems.